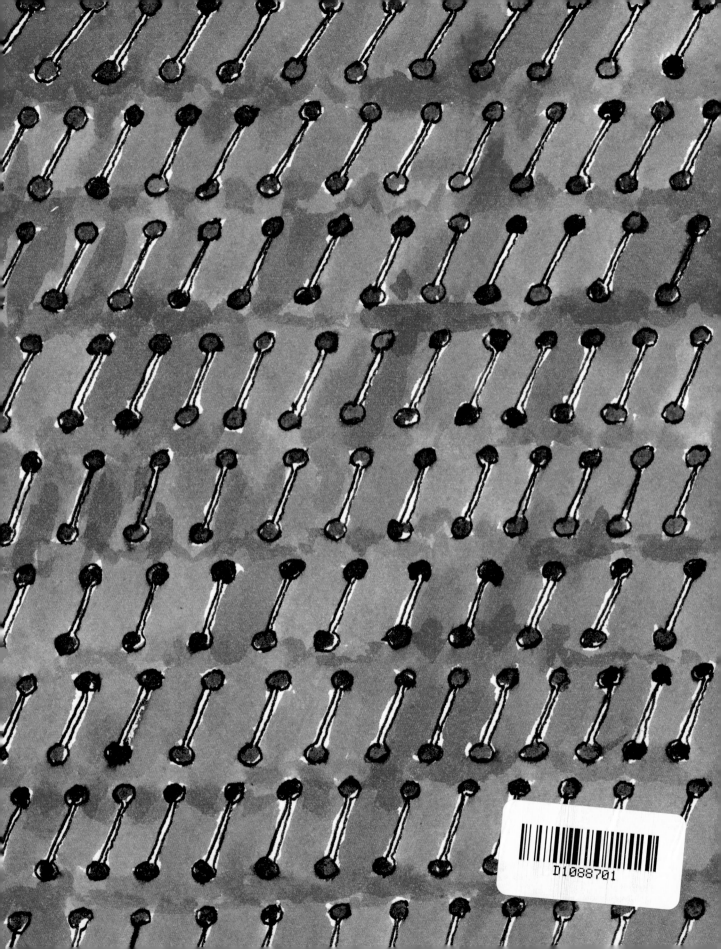

HENRY
GETS IN SHAPE

A HENRY DUCK BOOK

ROBERT QUACKENBUSH

ALADDIN NEW YORK LONDON TORONTO SYDNEY NEW DELHI

THIS ONE IS FOR

AIDAN AND EMMA.

ALADDIN
An imprint of Simon & Schuster Children's Publishing Division
1230 Avenue of the Americas, New York, New York 10020
This Aladdin hardcover edition August 2021
Copyright © 2021 by Robert Quackenbush
For information about special discounts for bulk purchases, please contact
Simon & Schuster Special Sales at 1-866-506-1949 or business@simonandschuster.com.
The Simon & Schuster Speakers Bureau can bring authors to your live event. For more
information or to book an event contact the Simon & Schuster Speakers Bureau
at 1-866-248-3049 or visit our website at www.simonspeakers.com.
Book designed by Tiara Iandiorio
The illustrations for this book were rendered in watercolor, pen, and ink.
The text of this book was set in Neutraface Slab Text.
Manufactured in China 0521 SCP
10 9 8 7 6 5 4 3 2 1
Library of Congress Control Number 2020939756
ISBN 978-1-5344-1562-1 (hc)
ISBN 978-1-5344-1564-5 (eBook)

ON THE DAY Henry the Duck was going to take his friend Clara to the movies, he stopped to weigh himself. He was surprised to see he weighed so much. He wanted to do something about it right away.

He ran to a store that sold gear for doing exercises. He bought an exercise bike, barbells, and a whole list of things for his workouts.

Then he went home to wait for the delivery of his goods.

When everything arrived, Henry

put on gym clothes and set to

work doing some exercises.

He started with the barbells.

But Henry got the heavy barbells
no higher than his chest when
they fell.

    Henry's feet were smashed!

Henry quit the barbells and sat down on a stool to rest his sore feet. He reached for a twisting bar to trim his waistline.

He began twisting back and forth with the pole on his shoulders.

Henry kept on twisting back and forth with the pole. He did not look where the pole was headed.

CRASH!

The pole destroyed Henry's brand-new TV!

Henry put down the twisting bar

and went to do chin-up exercises.

But first he had to nail the chinning

bar to his kitchen doorframe.

That done, he began doing

chin-ups.

Suddenly, the chinning bar broke away from the nails while Henry was on it.

Henry fell to the floor with a bang.

Henry quit the chinning bar and
went to the electric machine for
losing weight. He put the belt
around his waist and switched
on the machine.

At once, the machine tossed Henry
this way and that at full speed.
Henry got a tummy ache.

Quickly, he shut off the machine
and waited for his tummy to settle.

While he waited, he wondered
what kind of exercise he should
try next.

When he felt better, Henry thought jogging would be a safe and easy exercise. He put on his sneakers. Then he went outside.

Henry started to jog.

Suddenly, it began to pour down

rain. Henry got soaking wet.

He had to go back home.

Inside again, Henry took off his wet sneakers. Then he climbed on the exercise bike. He was sure that this would be the best way to do his workouts.

He started pedaling.

The bike wheel turned faster and faster. Soon the wheel was going faster than Henry could pedal. His feet got caught in the whirling pedals.

He got tossed off the bike!

So now Henry was sore all over.

But he remembered what the

scales on the street had said.

He decided to jump rope as

a way to exercise.

Henry began to jump. But as he jumped, he got tangled in the rope. Henry fell to the floor, tied up by the rope.

Henry worked his way across the room to his telephone and knocked it to the floor with his body. Then he tapped an emergency number on the telephone keypad with his beak.

When someone answered, he asked for a rescue squad to come and untie him.

That night Henry staggered to Clara's house to take her to the movies. But when Clara saw him, she said, "Why, Henry, you look out of shape. Let's forget the movies. What you need is . . .

Some exercise. Let's go dancing."

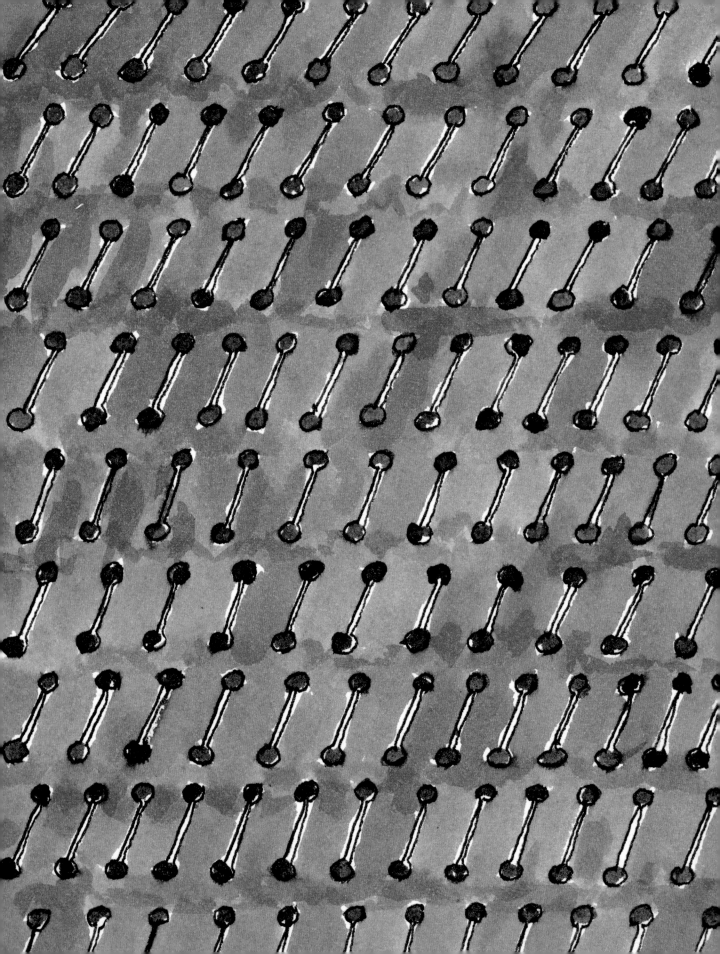